The Woodsman

by Steven Fechter

A SAMUEL FRENCH ACTING EDITION

SAMUEL FRENCH

FOUNDED 1830

NEW YORK HOLLYWOOD LONDON TORONTO

SAMUELFRENCH.COM

ISBN 978-0-573-69707-4   Printed in U.S.A.   #29073

IMPORTANT BILLING AND CREDIT
REQUIREMENTS

All producers of *THE WOODSMAN must* give credit to the Author of the Play in all programs distributed in connection with performances of the Play, and in all instances in which the title of the Play appears for the purposes of advertising, publicizing or otherwise exploiting the Play and/or a production. The name of the Author *must* appear on a separate line on which no other name appears, immediately following the title and *must* appear in size of type not less than fifty percent of the size of the title type.

THE WOODSMAN was first produced by The Actors Studio Free Theater at Raw Space, New York City, opening on March 1, 2000, with the following cast:

WALTER	Bernie Sheredy*
GIRL/ROBIN	Danielle Hildreth*
ROSEN	Marc Forget*
CARLOS	Antone Pagán*
NIKKI	Sue-Anne Morrow*
LUCAS	David W. Butler*

Directed by Sharon Fallon; set design by Derek Stenborg; costume design by Shelley Norton; lighting design by Jeff Croiter; sound design by Geoff Zink; production stage manager was Fran Rubenstein*; assistant director was Jennifer Spence
*Member Actors Equity

THE WOODSMAN was produced by Against the Grain Theatre Company at The Old Red Lion Theatre Pub, London, UK, opening on April 7, 2009, with the following cast:

WALTER	Richard Ings
GIRL/ROBIN	Emma Pollard
ROSEN	Dominic Coddington
CARLOS	Mark Philip Compton
NIKKI	Lisa Came
LUCAS	John Samuel Worsey

Directed by Stuart Watson; set and lighting design by Ben Sandford; costume design by Samantha Dew; sound design by Barney Hart Dyke; scenic artist was Tony Bennett; stage manager was Helena Tondryk; deputy stage managers were Jen Payne and Anthony Doran

CHARACTERS

WALTER – early 40s
GIRL – 12
ROSEN – early 30s
CARLOS – late 30s
NIKKI – early 30s
LUCAS – 40s
ROBIN – 11

Note: **GIRL** and **ROBIN** should be played by the same actor.

TIME

Present

PLACE

Walter's apartment, Rosen's office, a park

(On a bare stage are three wooden chairs: two center stage, one downstage right. WALTER, an average-built man, wearing khaki pants and a flannel shirt, sits center stage. He gazes into the audience.)

(A GIRL enters. She has long hair, wears a nightgown, and is barefoot. Her age is about 12. She stares at WALTER. We hear a faint sound that gets progressively louder. It is the sound of children – many children – screaming, screeching, and laughing. WALTER smiles. Then the sound abruptly stops. The GIRL exits.)

(ROSEN enters and sits in downstage chair. He is a boyish-looking man who speaks with genial animation.)

ROSEN. So. How are you adjusting?

(WALTER faces him.)

WALTER. I'm adjusting okay.

ROSEN. And your new apartment?

WALTER. The apartment's okay.

ROSEN. Are you taking your medication?

WALTER. It gives me headaches.

ROSEN. But you are taking it.

WALTER. Yeah.

ROSEN. Good.

(He writes in a notepad.)

I'll talk to your physician about the headaches. Perhaps he can change the prescription.

WALTER. Thanks.

ROSEN. How's your job at the warehouse?

WALTER. The job's okay.

ROSEN. Do I take "okay" to mean you feel good about working there?

WALTER. I said the job's okay.

ROSEN. That's right, you did.

    (pause)

    Have you made any friends there?

WALTER. I'm not running for Mr. Popularity.

ROSEN. *(beat)* You seem a little hostile today.

WALTER. That was a joke. It's called sarcasm, Dr. Rosen.

ROSEN. No need to call me doctor. I'm a therapist not a psychiatrist.

WALTER. It's all the same.

ROSEN. You don't like coming here, do you?

WALTER. It's okay.

ROSEN. But you don't like coming here. Be honest, Walter.

WALTER. Honest? No.

ROSEN. Good! That was an honest answer. And why don't you like coming here?

WALTER. Honest? Your cheery personality makes my skin itch.

ROSEN. *(stung)* Is it just my cheery personality that makes your skin itch?

WALTER. Forget it.

ROSEN. Maybe it's the way I look. Or the sound of my name. Do you find my name irritating?

WALTER. Rosen? I don't have a problem with that.

ROSEN. Because if you did, I know a therapist named Ryan. I also know a therapist named Chung.

WALTER. I don't need someone else.

ROSEN. Fine.

WALTER. Anti-Semitism is not my problem.

ROSEN. No.

    (**WALTER** *looks at* **ROSEN.**)

WALTER. You okay, Rosen?

ROSEN. I'm fine.

WALTER. Honest?

ROSEN. To be honest, no. I've been trying to reconnect with my Jewish identity of late. It's made me a bit hypersensitive. I'm sorry.

WALTER. Forget it.

ROSEN. Last week I found out that an aunt of mine died in Auschwitz. She was just a girl.

WALTER. You got a first name, Rosen?

ROSEN. Ira.

WALTER. I'll stick with Rosen.

ROSEN. Walter, I'd like you to do something when you're at home.

WALTER. What's that?

ROSEN. I'd like you to keep a journal.

WALTER. You mean like a diary?

ROSEN. That's right.

WALTER. No way.

ROSEN. Why not?

WALTER. Diaries have sent too many guys to prison.

ROSEN. I don't understand.

WALTER. Ev-i-dence.

ROSEN. It never crossed my mind.

WALTER. Of course.

ROSEN. It was just an idea.

WALTER. Bad idea.

ROSEN. I thought a journal would encourage you to reflect.

WALTER. Reflect.

ROSEN. That's right.

WALTER. You think reflection is good.

ROSEN. It's very good, indeed.

WALTER. How's that?

ROSEN. By reflection we can derive a deeper meaning from our experience in life. We gain greater understanding about ourselves that can lead to making better choices in our relationships, our careers, and our goals.

WALTER. You read that in a book.

(ROSEN *doesn't respond.*)

What if I lied in my journal? Just made up a lot of shit.

ROSEN. To write a conscious lie, you first have to reflect on what you believe is true. I don't care by what process you go about it.

WALTER. You kill me, Rosen.

ROSEN. Come on, Walter, what do you say?

WALTER. *(pause)* I don't know. Keeping a diary always seemed egotistical to me. Writing about yourself like you're the center of the universe. Most of the time it's just a lot of whining.

ROSEN. Some of our greatest writers and thinkers kept journals: Saint Augustine, Rousseau, Virginia Woolf.

WALTER. Whining is whining.

ROSEN. Try it for a week. See what happens.

WALTER. No fucking way.

ROSEN. Then just think about it.

(ROSEN *exits.* WALTER *remains in his chair. From his pocket he takes out a small notebook and a pen. The lights fade to half. He opens the notebook to the first page. He writes a line then crosses it out, cursing under his breath. He stares into space.*)

WALTER. Kirby? Yeah, Kirby.

(*He writes on cover.*)

You're not going to like this Kirb, but I am naming my journal after you. See, you were the biggest, meanest sonofabitch I ever met in the pen. But, man, I could tell you anything. I was real sorry when I heard you did yourself in.

(*pause*)

Okay, Kirby. Here's the deal. I talk, I write, you listen. And this isn't going to be about whining. No bullshit about how nobody understood me and life is stupid and unfair. None of that crap. This is just going to be whatever's in my head.

(pause)

Now, where am I going to hide you, Kirb?

(He looks around but sees nothing he likes. Offstage there is the sound of a loud "thud." Lights up full.)

(CARLOS enters carrying a small wooden table. WALTER sticks notebook down his back pocket. CARLOS is a hispanic man in working clothes.)

CARLOS. This little table is one heavy bitch.

WALTER. Cherry.

CARLOS. Huh?

WALTER. Just put it over there.

(CARLOS sets it down up-center stage.)

It's made from cherry. That's a hard wood. Some of the best cabinetwork is made from the wood of wild black cherry. That's what this table's made from.

(The men look at the table.)

CARLOS. It's a nice table.

WALTER. See how fine the grain is? Look how deep and rich the red runs. The wood still pulses with life. It's like when you look at this table you don't see a piece of furniture…you see a living thing.

CARLOS. Yeah. It's really nice.

WALTER. I went to half a dozen lumber yards and drove a hundred miles before I found the right wood. It's my own design. You won't find another table like it in the world.

CARLOS. It was a beautiful wedding present.

WALTER. Then why the fuck are you giving it back to me?

CARLOS. You need a table.

WALTER. She was going to throw it out, wasn't she? Just toss it like scrap wood.

CARLOS. It wasn't like that.

WALTER. Then what? What!

CARLOS. She's got all this new furniture now. What do you call it? Santa Fe? Southwest? That Indian shit. She's filled the entire house. I liked the old stuff better. It was comfortable. I could put my feet on it. But Annette's like obsessed – crazy! You know how she gets. So this table…Annette says to me, Carlos, this don't fit anymore with the new stuff. She says, give it to Goodwill. But I kept it in the attic. I thought maybe you'd like it.

WALTER. But she would have thrown it out if you didn't hide it.

CARLOS. I didn't hide it, Walter. She knew it was there.

(He rubs the top of the table.)

It's a nice table. I couldn't give it away.

WALTER. I made that table for you and Annette. I put a lot of love and work into it.

CARLOS. I know, man, I know. I love this table too. But I also love my wife.

(He walks downstage and looks into audience.)

Hey, is that a school?

WALTER. What do you think?

CARLOS. It looks like a school.

WALTER. K through sixth.

CARLOS. I didn't notice it when I parked.

(He shakes his head.)

Living across the street from a grade school. Jesus.

WALTER. Something wrong with that?

CARLOS. I was just thinking…of the noise.

WALTER. Maybe that's why the rent's so cheap.

CARLOS. I bet it gets damn noisy.

WALTER. I like the noise.

CARLOS. All those screaming kids? I wouldn't like it. We live on a quiet block. I like the quiet.

(WALTER moves downstage.)

WALTER. In the morning I see them walking down the street. Some move like sleepwalkers, others hop around like pogo sticks. They sound like a thousand chirping sparrows. In the afternoon they spill out of the building. You should see them…shrieking with laughter, tripping over each other to get out. It's as if they were let out of prison. I can understand that. But then a few of them don't look so happy going home. And I can understand that too.

CARLOS. You still talk like a crazy poet.

WALTER. The sound of children is the sound of life, Carlos. The sound of grown-ups is the sound of death. I prefer life.

CARLOS. I'm just thinking that maybe it's not so healthy being this close. You know, to a school.

WALTER. You sound like my parole officer.

CARLOS. Bet he wasn't too happy about your apartment's location.

WALTER. She.

(mimics parole officer)

You are not supposed to come within one hundred feet of places where children congregate.

(his voice)

I'm not supposed to what, ma'am?

(her voice)

Come within one hundred feet.

(his voice)

Do what within a hundred feet?

(her voice)

Come! Come!

*(**CARLOS** laughs.)*

Is she a dim bulb or what?

CARLOS. And she still let you live here?

WALTER. So then I say, all sweet and earnest, "You find me a clean and decent place for three hundred dollars a month, and I will move there. Can you find such a place in this town?" Well, that shut her up.

(pause)

I measured it.

CARLOS. You what?

WALTER. I measured the distance from my window to the school. At night – one foot in front of the other. My building's a hundred and five feet from the school's entrance. But when you include the height of my third-floor apartment, I'm one hundred and thirty feet.

CARLOS. *(laughs)* What'd you do, walk up the side of the building like a human fly?

WALTER. I figured it out. The apartments have eight-foot ceilings. Multiply that by three floors. You don't need to be a builder to know that.

CARLOS. Man, you were a terrific builder.

WALTER. You don't have to say that.

CARLOS. Everyone said it – "That Walter can build any-thing."

*(***WALTER*** is silent.)*

I mean, what's to stop you from being one again?

WALTER. References.

(pause)

Still with the same company?

CARLOS. Sure. I'll never forget you got me started there.

WALTER. I just recommended you. You still had to prove yourself.

CARLOS. I'm a foreman now.

WALTER. No shit.

CARLOS. Five years now.

WALTER. Beautiful. How's business?

CARLOS. Booming. Lots of building going on. We can't keep up with all the work. In fact, I just hired a few new guys…just until we catch up.

(The men are silent a moment.)

Gotta go. Your sister worries. And when she worries, she yells. I like a quiet house.

WALTER. You're a good friend, Carlos. The only one in my family who still talks to me.

CARLOS. I remember when they all referred to me as "the little spic poor Annette married." Except her brother. You treated me with respect.

(pause)

Look, you paid your dues. Your slate is clean now.

WALTER. What about Annette?

CARLOS. I'm working on her. She'll come around.

WALTER. Is it because of Anna?

CARLOS. I don't know. Annette won't talk about it.

(pause)

When you got in trouble...it killed her. It was like somebody had smashed a beautiful crystal statue she owned.

WALTER. I know she suffered.

CARLOS. She was crazy about your wife and kid. She and Helen were like sisters, the way they were always laughing and shit.

WALTER. *(pause)* You ever hear...

CARLOS. We haven't heard from Helen since she left – about ten years ago. A year later, she sent us a postcard from Denver. Said she was moving to Oregon. That was it.

WALTER. She never wrote me a line, not counting the divorce papers. My little girl was seven.

(pause)

If I saw my daughter now I probably wouldn't know her.

CARLOS. Helen was a good Catholic girl – like your sister.

WALTER. How old is Anna?

CARLOS. *(grins)* She'll be twelve next week! We're throwing a big birthday party on Saturday. Wish I could ask you to come – to the party.

WALTER. Only if it's no closer than a hundred feet.

(beat)

Bad joke.

CARLOS. You should see her. She is so pretty.

(**WALTER** *is silent.*)

Hey, you want to see a picture of her?

WALTER. Nah, that's okay.

CARLOS. I've got a picture right in my wallet.

(He reaches into his back pocket.)

WALTER. Don't want to see any goddamn picture.

CARLOS. That's cool. Whenever. I mean, I got hundreds of pictures of her. Plus hours of video. She's my treasure.

(gets worked up)

It's hard to explain, but she's like one of those girls in fairy tales. You know, like Snow White, except she's smart as a fox.

(laughs)

I get silly when I talk about Anna.

(**WALTER** *walks away from* **CARLOS**.)

I remember when she was a little thing and I'd give her baths. I'd hold her wet little body in my hands and think, can anything be more perfect? She's the light of my life.

WALTER. Don't love her too much, Carlos.

CARLOS. No such thing, man. I couldn't love her enough.

(awkward silence)

Guess I'd better go.

WALTER. Yeah.

(They stiffly embrace.)

CARLOS. I'll come by in a few days.

(He exits. WALTER runs his hand along the table top, then he sits. Lights fade to half. The sound of children at play fades in. WALTER takes out his notebook and starts writing.)

WALTER. Hey, Kirby. A funny thing is going on below. I told you that I watch the kids arrive at school in the morning. Sit by the window, drink my coffee, smoke a cigarette, then go to work.

(Pause. He writes.)

For the last few weeks I've noticed someone else watching them. How should I describe him? Twenties. Clean cut. Pleasant face. Good build, like he works out regular. Nice clothes. The pants always creased.

(Pause. He writes.)

I see him talk to the boys. Fifth and sixth graders. He goes for the pretty ones. Slender bodies with faces like angels. He offers them candy. Big bars of Snickers, Baby Ruths, Milky Ways, Butterfingers. It's why I call him Candy. Every Tuesday and Thursday he's there.

(Pause. He writes.)

Candy drives a white Volvo that he parks a block away. He hasn't taken any of the boys to his car. Not yet. He's working on it. Or maybe he's fighting it. It's all the same. For now Candy's just happy to look. To talk. To touch. I see him rest his hand on a boy's shoulder as he gives him a Hershey Bar. The boy doesn't notice the hand. He will when it rubs the back of his neck.

(He looks at notebook.)

So what would you do, Kirb? If you were me. Call the cops? Yeah, that's pretty funny. Besides, Candy hasn't broken any laws. But what if he seduces a little angel to go for a ride in his car? What then?

(He writes.)

I hear you. I'm not going to call the cops. If the boy goes in the car it's because he wants to go in the car.

(Lights up full. The sound stops. **WALTER** *puts journal away in table drawer.* **ROSEN** *enters and sits in down stage chair.)*

ROSEN. How do you feel about that?

*(***WALTER*** *faces him.)*

WALTER. I don't feel anything.

ROSEN. You have no feelings for your niece?

WALTER. She was born after they put me away. How can I have feelings?

ROSEN. Then why are you talking about this?

WALTER. Gotta talk about something.

ROSEN. What are you afraid will happen?

WALTER. I'm not afraid. I'm just saying that Carlos has a thing for his daughter, and if he isn't careful he's going to suffer.

ROSEN. And you don't want him to suffer.

WALTER. I like Carlos. He's been real decent to me.

ROSEN. Have you talked to Carlos about your concerns?

WALTER. I'm not that crazy.

ROSEN. Do you think you're crazy?

WALTER. If I'm not then what the hell am I doing here?

ROSEN. Why do you think you're here?

WALTER. You know why. It's part of the parole deal.

ROSEN. Is that what you're angry about?

WALTER. Talking to you is like riding on a merry-go-round.

ROSEN. That is a marvelous image, Walter.

(moves his hand in a circle)

Because by going in circles we find the things we missed the first time around.

WALTER. How long is this going to take?

ROSEN. *(checks his watch)* We have a few more minutes.

WALTER. I mean my cure.

ROSEN. Your cure?

WALTER. Right.

ROSEN. We have a lot of work to do.

WALTER. Will I ever be normal?

ROSEN. How's the journal?

WALTER. I'm still thinking about it.

ROSEN. I wish you'd give it a try.

WALTER. You didn't answer my question.

ROSEN. I'm sorry. What was the question?

WALTER. *(speaks slowly)* Will I ever be normal?

ROSEN. I couldn't say.

WALTER. You couldn't say.

ROSEN. I'm afraid not.

WALTER. Do you know what "normal" is?

ROSEN. I suppose it's however society defines it.

WALTER. How do you define it?

ROSEN. I don't.

WALTER. Then how do you know if your patients are getting better?

ROSEN. They usually tell me.

WALTER. How do they know?

ROSEN. *(pause)* What is your idea of being normal?

WALTER. *(mimics* **ROSEN***)* What is your idea of being a Jew?

ROSEN. *(looks at watch)* Why don't we continue this on Thursday.

WALTER. I want to be normal!

ROSEN. Then go see a therapist who will tell you you're normal.

WALTER. Fuck you, Rosen!

ROSEN. I know –

WALTER. You don't know!

ROSEN. I know you're frustrated, Walter, but you really are making...

(*WALTER gets up and moves away.*)

...progress.

(*ROSEN exits. WALTER walks over to the table. He grabs the table's legs. With great effort he slowly lifts the table to the level of his head. The GIRL enters and stands behind WALTER.*)

GIRL. Wallie.

(*WALTER's arms start shaking. He lowers the table down, slumps in a chair, buries his head in his hands.*)

(*NIKKI enters. The GIRL exits, passing NIKKI who walks downstage. She has short hair, wears black jeans, tank top, black leather jacket, and heavy work boots. She has numerous pierced earrings in each ear. She looks into the audience.*)

NIKKI. Southern light.

WALTER. (*lifts his head*) What?

NIKKI. Your windows face south. Northern light is purest. But southern light is very good.

WALTER. I'll buy a plant.

NIKKI. You should. You should buy a few plants. I've got shitty light in my place, but my plants don't seem to mind. Light's important, but it's not everything. Is that a school?

WALTER. K through sixth.

NIKKI. Doesn't it get noisy?

WALTER. I like the noise.

NIKKI. My place faces a truck street. Eighteen-wheelers bouncing into potholes the size of canyons. I've got cracks in every window from the shaking.

WALTER. You must hate it.

NIKKI. I go backpacking a lot. Lose myself in wilderness for a week or two. Get away from man-made noise. Sleep on the ground, bathe in waterfalls, stare at the stars and planets. I don't use a tent – don't believe in them. Less to carry too.

WALTER. What about bears?

NIKKI. What about them?

WALTER. They could eat you.

NIKKI. *(laughs)* If a bear wanted me, a tent wouldn't exactly deter him. Surprised to see me?

WALTER. I didn't think you were serious.

NIKKI. I am a serious woman.

WALTER. Something to drink?

NIKKI. What have you got?

WALTER. I've got cheap South American wine.

NIKKI. From Chile?

WALTER. Paraguay. You can still taste the tin mines.

NIKKI. Sure.

> *(WALTER exits. NIKKI takes her jacket off and throws it over a chair. On her right shoulder is a tattoo – a pair of breasts with angel wings. She looks around.)*

There's something wrong with this picture.

> *(WALTER reenters with a bottle of red wine and glasses.)*

WALTER. You don't like my Van Gogh calendar?

NIKKI. I'm talking about you.

WALTER. Me?

> *(He brings wine and glasses to table.)*

NIKKI. You seem like a nice, intelli –

WALTER. Don't forget sensitive.

NIKKI. Shut up and let me finish. Here's this nice, intelligent, and sensitive guy. He works in a warehouse, loading and unloading furniture, and lives alone in the ghetto. Very weird.

WALTER. No weirder than a sharp, young, good-looking woman working in a warehouse, loading and unloading furniture.

NIKKI. What's weird about that?

> *(WALTER pours wine.)*

WALTER. I heard they offered you a sales job and you turned it down.

(She doesn't reply.)

That true?

NIKKI. Where'd you hear that?

WALTER. The usual grapevine.

NIKKI. That bimbo secretary has a mouth like an open sewer pipe: A lot of shit runs out of it.

WALTER. Is it true?

NIKKI. *(pause)* Yes.

WALTER. So, why'd you turn it down?

NIKKI. I don't like to deal with the public. I don't like wearing skirts; I don't like wearing makeup; and I don't like standing around with a pasted smile on my face for eight fucking hours a day.

WALTER. Somehow, I don't see you with a pasted smile.

(He hands her a glass of wine.)

Here's to weird lives and cheap wine.

(He raises his glass, they drink. They both make a face.)

God, that's awful.

NIKKI. It is, but you're trying to put me off.

WALTER. Am I?

NIKKI. You're quiet at work.

WALTER. I'm just quiet.

NIKKI. You don't hang out with the other guys.

WALTER. Neither do you.

NIKKI. You're putting me off again.

WALTER. Just making an observation.

NIKKI. They're all jerks.

(She takes a large swallow of wine which almost makes her gag.)

WALTER. They're not bad.

NIKKI. Not bad? You don't hear what I hear.

WALTER. What do you hear?

NIKKI. Cunt. Twat. Slit. Slash. Crack. "Bitch" when they're feeling generous.

(She slams her glass down on table.)

Fucking pricks! They don't think I hear them.

WALTER. It's just talk. They don't know what to make of you.

NIKKI. What's the problem? I dress like the guys. I sweat like the guys. I work as hard as any guy, and I can lift as much as most of the guys. If it helps, I'll stuff a fucking sock down my pants.

*(**WALTER** looks amused.)*

I also hear what they call you.

WALTER. Don't tell me! I still have to work with them.

(He gets up and walks downstage. He takes a sip of wine, makes a face.)

Damn.

*(**NIKKI** gets up and walks toward him.)*

NIKKI. So what do you make of me?

WALTER. What do you mean?

NIKKI. You invited me to come over. Remember? This afternoon. Now I'm over.

WALTER. We were talking…having our lunch…eating sandwiches.

NIKKI. You never spoke to me before. How come?

WALTER. I thought you were a dyke.

*(**NIKKI** laughs.)*

Are you?

NIKKI. What do you think?

WALTER. You acted like you might be one. I thought you looked…good. But still…

NIKKI. Do you still think I'm a dyke?

WALTER. If you were you wouldn't be here.

NIKKI. Unless I came to lure you into bed so I could cut your dick off.

WALTER. *(looks startled then slowly grins)* Nah. If you did you wouldn't have told me.

(pause)

So, are you a dyke?

NIKKI. I've got friends who are.

WALTER. Your friends aren't here. You are. More wine?

NIKKI. Sure.

(WALTER pours wine into glasses.)

I used to think you were just shy. But I think it's something else.

WALTER. What?

NIKKI. You're damaged. Something happened to you.

(WALTER is silent.)

I'm not easily shocked.

WALTER. I got that impression.

NIKKI. So…what's your dark secret?

WALTER. Why do you want to know?

(NIKKI moves close to him.)

NIKKI. Don't you think I should know before we have sex?

(WALTER looks surprised.)

I don't like to waste time. Your wine sucks, and this neighborhood's too dicey for a second get-acquainted visit.

(She kisses him.)

You could be a serial killer. One of those guys who has sex with young women then, at the moment of climax, slashes their throats, dismembers them, and devours their reproductive organs.

WALTER. Now I'm shocked.

NIKKI. Good.

(kisses him again)

Are you going to tell me your dark secret before we have sex?

(WALTER kisses her.)

WALTER. No.

NIKKI. *(shrugs)* Okay.

(She takes off her tank top and exits. **WALTER** *starts to follow her then stops. He doesn't see* **ROSEN** *enter. He has a yellow Star of David pinned to his sports coat.)*

ROSEN. She's waiting for you.

*(***WALTER** *turns and stares at him.)*

WALTER. What the hell are you doing here?

ROSEN. You called me.

WALTER. Bullshit.

ROSEN. *(points to his head)* In here you did.

WALTER. *(looks at* **ROSEN***'s chest)* What's with the star?

ROSEN. That was your idea.

WALTER. What are you talking about?

ROSEN. Feelings of persecution…the fear of extinction… dehumanization. The yellow Star of David has become an icon of all that and more. Personally I find it tacky, but it's your projection. Now, what's the problem?

WALTER. What should I do?

ROSEN. What do you want to do?

WALTER. Go in there and…

ROSEN. Have sex?

WALTER. Yes.

ROSEN. Then what's the problem?

WALTER. Sex.

ROSEN. What kind of sex are we talking about?

WALTER. Regular sex. Normal sex. I want to have normal sex!

ROSEN. What's stopping you?

WALTER. It's been a long time since I had normal sex with a woman.

ROSEN. One doesn't forget.

WALTER. I'm afraid…I'll fuck it up.

ROSEN. Walter, I think you're a little hung up on the word "normal."

WALTER. I need guidance, damnit!

ROSEN. *(He puts his finger to his lips.)* Shhh. Just go in there and do what feels natural. And don't ask me what "natural" is. What's natural for me may be bizarre to somebody else.

WALTER. What kind of sex do you have?

ROSEN. *(looks at his watch)* Your time is up.

WALTER. Hey, I called you.

(points to his head)

In here.

ROSEN. You think you're the only patient who imagines my help?

*(He exits. **WALTER** stands there a moment. Then he grabs the bottle of wine and exits. Blackout.)*

*(Long pause. Lights up. **WALTER** and **NIKKI** sit at the table. **WALTER** wears his pants but no shirt. **NIKKI** wears **WALTER**'s shirt but no pants.)*

WALTER. So you're not a dyke.

NIKKI. Not tonight.

(smiles)

Hey, that was...interesting.

WALTER. What?

(She gives him a look.)

Oh yeah. I guess I'm a bit unorthodox.

NIKKI. That's an understatement.

WALTER. You're still here.

NIKKI. I didn't say I didn't enjoy it.

WALTER. It's the only way I can...

NIKKI. I bet we can find other ways.

WALTER. I'm a little wrung out now.

NIKKI. Whoa. I didn't mean like this second.

WALTER. Of course. Sorry. I'm such a fucking asshole.

NIKKI. No you're not.

WALTER. Don't tell me I'm not a fucking asshole when I know I'm a fucking asshole!

(He gets up and walks downstage.)

NIKKI. What's the problem?

WALTER. You think I have a problem?

NIKKI. Do you?

WALTER. It's been a while.

NIKKI. How long is a while?

WALTER. Twelve years.

NIKKI. Twelve years? Wow. That is beautiful. Were you in some kind of monastery?

WALTER. Yeah, something like that.

NIKKI. Tell me about it.

WALTER. Maybe later.

NIKKI. How about in the morning?

WALTER. The morning?

NIKKI. I thought I'd stay the night.

WALTER. What for?

NIKKI. Well, Walter, this is going to sound off-the-wall, but I like to sleep with a man after we fuck.

(WALTER is silent.)

Did I say something wrong?

WALTER. I suffer from insomnia.

NIKKI. Is that all?

WALTER. When I do sleep I sweat a lot. Usually I get nightmares and wake up screaming.

NIKKI. I sleep like a dead horse. Anything else?

WALTER. *(embarrassed)* The sheets need washing.

NIKKI. We'll turn the sheets over – or we won't use them at all.

(She takes WALTER's hand and leads him off stage. Blackout. Pause. Spot on WALTER downstage staring into audience.)

WALTER. *(in the ratatat tone of a sportscaster)* Good morning, Kirby and fellow sports fans. The match is about to begin. The kids parade down the sidewalk heading for

school. Candy enters the arena looking fit and trim.
He checks out the scene but plays it cool. He's defi-
nitely holding back.

(pause)

Uh-oh, Candy's eyes have locked onto something. Oh
yeah. Trailing behind the others is a delicate cherub of
a lad who has separated from his friends. Candy quickly
makes his move. He pats the cherub on his head and
ruffles his hair. With his other hand he offers the boy a
bag of M&Ms. Jumbo size. The boy tears open the bag.
Round one to Candy.

(We hear clang of a boxing bell.)

Candy points across the street to his white Volvo. A very
risky move by Candy to park his car so close. However,
the boy walks away. Round two goes to the cherub.

(clang of bell)

Undeterred, Candy struts around the boy, rapping,
clapping, snapping his fingers. I have never seen
him act so cocky. Candy points to his car again then
dances slow-mo toward it. The cherub looks at Candy;
the cherub looks at the car; the cherub looks for his
friends. But his friends are long gone. The cherub is
alone. The cherub crosses the street.

(normal tone)

The cherub gets in the car.

(pause)

NIKKI *(Offstage)* What did you do?

(lights up full)

WALTER. Nothing.

> *(**NIKKI** enters dressed in her own clothes. She tosses him
> his shirt. As he puts it on she walks downstage and looks
> out the "window.")*

Sleep well?

*(He exits. **NIKKI** stretches.)*

NIKKI. Like a dead horse. You?

WALTER *(Offstage)* Not bad. Just one screaming nightmare.

NIKKI. So what did you do?

*(**WALTER** returns with two mugs of coffee. He sets them on the table.)*

WALTER. I hope you like it black. I don't have any milk.

(She goes to the table. They sit.)

NIKKI. Walter.

WALTER. It's Mexican instant.

NIKKI. Walter.

WALTER. It's bitter, but it's strong. You want milk, I'll go out and –

NIKKI. Hey!

WALTER. What?

NIKKI. We had sex. I slept with you. I didn't cut your dick off. And you didn't eat my reproductive organs.

WALTER. *(winces)* Wish you wouldn't say that.

NIKKI. Don't you think you can tell me your dark secret?

*(**WALTER** is silent. **NIKKI** kisses him.)*

I won't run away. Promise.

WALTER. What's the worst thing you ever did?

NIKKI. The worst?

WALTER. Yeah.

NIKKI. *(considers as she sips her coffee)* Fucked my best friend's husband. I mean a friend since the second grade. Her husband was hot for me and, God, was he cute. But still, I shouldn't have done it.

(pause)

He had a beautiful body. No chest hair, which usually turns me off, but on him it looked fine. She was an international flight attendant. So we'd go at it for days like wild ponies while she was in some country we couldn't pronounce.

(pause)

Then he told her, the shit. Why do men do that? It broke up our friendship, broke up their marriage. I still feel like the evilest woman alive when I think of it.

(looks at him)

So what did you do?

WALTER. *(stares at his mug)* I molested little girls.

NIKKI. Molested little girls.

WALTER. Yeah.

NIKKI. *(laughs)* That's funny.

WALTER. You don't believe me?

(She laughs harder.)

I wish the judge had your sense of humor.

NIKKI. *(quiets down)* You're not joking?

WALTER. Twelve years in prison is no joke.

*(**NIKKI** stares at **WALTER**.)*

Look, why don't you go? I'll see you at work.

(She doesn't move.)

NIKKI. How many girls did you molest?

WALTER. Obviously one too many.

(brief laugh)

Sorry.

NIKKI. What did you do to them?

WALTER. This can't possibly interest you.

NIKKI. Yes.

*(**WALTER** gets up and walks downstage.)*

Yes!

WALTER. It's not what you think. I was gentle.

NIKKI. How young?

WALTER. Between ten and twelve. Once a nine-year-old told me she was eleven. Once a fourteen-year-old told me she was twelve. I always asked how old they were.

*(**NIKKI** looks shaken.)*

NIKKI. So it was mostly fondling? Shit like that?

WALTER. I never hurt them...never.

NIKKI. Twelve years in prison?

WALTER. The judge had a thing about sex offenders. Later I heard that his daughter had been raped. If I hadn't had a good lawyer it would have been twenty-five to thirty.

(He gazes out the window.)

I'll see you at work, okay?

NIKKI. Okay.

(Pause. She doesn't move.)

WALTER. Still here?

NIKKI. What was prison like?

WALTER. You don't really –

NIKKI. Yes! I want to know.

WALTER. *(pause)* Prison is...time.

NIKKI. You mean the time you're locked away.

WALTER. No. Prison is time. That's it. That's all prison is – not about violent prisoners, abusive guards, enclosed spaces, not about any of that shit. It's just time. You think time, you feel time, you hear time. Your heart doesn't beat to live...it just beats time.

NIKKI. I'm sorry, Walter.

WALTER. Don't be sorry for me. I did those things. I'm dealing with that.

NIKKI. Is that why you like me to...do those things?

WALTER. I don't know.

NIKKI. It's okay.

WALTER. It's not okay!

NIKKI. I told you I'm not easily shocked.

WALTER. You should be shocked. Or do you get off on this shit?

NIKKI. What?

WALTER. Get your kicks somewhere else.

NIKKI. Hey, I'm not –

WALTER. Depraved? My mistake.

NIKKI. Walter –

WALTER. *(raises his fist)* Get the fuck out of here!

(She doesn't move. He sits, his anger spent.)

I had this plan once...or maybe it was a dream. I was going to quit the building business...open my own shop. Make and design fine country furniture. I had saved enough money...found the perfect place. Two thousand square feet. Cheap five-year-lease. The bank loan was in the bag. My wife was a hundred percent behind it. Everything was set...Then I got in trouble. You know what the worst kind of trouble is?

NIKKI. No.

WALTER. It's trouble you bring on the people you love the most.

NIKKI. I said I wouldn't run away.

WALTER. So you did.

NIKKI. You don't molest little girls anymore, do you?

WALTER. No! Never again. I swear to God.

NIKKI. See you at work?

(WALTER doesn't answer. NIKKI exits. The GIRL enters. The sound of children fades in louder and louder. WALTER is very still.)

GIRL. Wallie? What are you doing?

(The sound stops. She runs offstage before WALTER can catch sight of her. ROSEN enters and sits.)

ROSEN. You're very late.

WALTER. Sorry.

ROSEN. Please don't do it again.

WALTER. I said I was sorry.

ROSEN. I can't move my patients around to accommodate one person.

(WALTER stares at his hands.)

Luckily the next appointment cancelled.

WALTER. There's this...

ROSEN. Excuse me.

(He exits. **WALTER,** *still staring at his hands, doesn't notice he's left.)*

WALTER. ...this girl. I see...this girl. Not a real girl. She's in the back of my brain...just out of sight. I never see her ...but I know when she's near me...

*(***ROSEN*** reenters and sits.)*

ROSEN. Sorry.

*(***WALTER*** stares at him.)*

I needed to reschedule the cancellation. So, any problems?

WALTER. I got no problems. Except the new medication gives me the runs.

ROSEN. I'll call your physician. Anything else?

WALTER. Nope.

ROSEN. Fine.

(pause)

Walter, I want to ask you a question. I think it's an important question. Not so much important, but central. Will you try to answer it?

WALTER. If you ever get around to asking.

ROSEN. When did it all start?

WALTER. You mean my problem?

ROSEN. If by "problem" you mean your desire for pre-pubescent girls, yes.

WALTER. I don't know.

ROSEN. That's not a helpful answer.

WALTER. That's my answer.

ROSEN. Close your eyes.

WALTER. What?

ROSEN. I'd like you to close your eyes.

WALTER. Why?

ROSEN. To relax.

WALTER. *(snaps)* I'm relaxed.

ROSEN. Close your eyes and let your mind be a blank.

WALTER. Hey, Rosen, you going to hypnotize me?

ROBIN. No, I am not going to –

WALTER. Rosen the Magnificent!

ROSEN. I don't really go into that flash-and-trash stuff.

WALTER. *(closes his eyes)* Okay. Eyes closed, mind a blank. I'm all yours. Do it, Rosen.

(**ROSEN** *stands up and walks downstage.*)

ROSEN. When I say the word "girl" what is the earliest image that you can remember?

WALTER. The earliest image…Nothing. Can I open my eyes?

ROSEN. No. When I say the word "girl," when I say the word "pretty," when I say the word "pleasure" what is the earliest memory you see?

WALTER. *(eyes still closed)* I don't see –

ROSEN. In your mind, Walter. Take your time.

WALTER. *(Long pause. Surprised.)* I see my sister.

ROSEN. Which one?

WALTER. I only got one. Annette.

ROSEN. *(excited)* Where is she? What is she doing? Where are you? How old –

WALTER. Not so fast.

ROSEN. Sorry.

(*He moves upstage.*)

Where is she?

WALTER. In my bedroom.

ROSEN. What is she doing?

WALTER. Sleeping.

ROSEN. Where are you?

WALTER. I'm in bed too.

ROSEN. In this memory how old are you and Annette?

WALTER. We're little kids.

ROSEN. But exactly how old?

WALTER. I'm maybe about six…which would make her four.

(ROSEN *moves behind* WALTER.)

ROSEN. What are you doing in bed?

WALTER. Just lying there…We're taking a nap.

ROSEN. A nap?

WALTER. Little kids do that. You ever take a nap, Rosen?

ROSEN. Let's talk about your nap.

(WALTER *opens his eyes.*)

WALTER. I don't want to talk about it anymore.

(*He sees* ROSEN *behind him.*)

What the hell you doin' there?

ROSEN. Did you and your sister often take naps together?

WALTER. *(explodes)* I want you back in your chair! Right now!

ROSEN. All right.

(ROSEN *returns in his chair.*)

WALTER. Don't you ever do that again!

ROBIN. I won't.

WALTER. I don't like nobody behind my back!

ROSEN. Walter, what did you do while taking a nap with your sister?

WALTER. Nothing.

ROSEN. Did you touch her? Did you take off her clothes? Did you take off your clothes?

WALTER. This is garbage!

ROSEN. I'm only asking questions.

WALTER. Okay. I'll tell you what I did – just to shut you up.

(*pause*)

I smelled her hair.

ROSEN. What else?

WALTER. That's all. I just liked smelling her hair.

ROSEN. You felt pleasure.

WALTER. Yes.

(ROSEN *writes a few notes.*)

ROSEN. Did you get an erection?

WALTER. I was six years old!

ROSEN. I meant later…when you two took naps.

(WALTER *is silent.*)

When the two of you held each other. When you were ten or eleven and she was eight or nine. When your parents were out and the two of you were alone…completely alone in that big house.

WALTER. It was a small house.

ROSEN. All right. A small house…with small rooms.

WALTER. Where are you trying to go with this?

(ROSEN *puts his pen down.*)

ROSEN. I still remember getting a raging hard-on in the sixth grade from just looking at Martha D'Angelo. The first girl in my class with breasts. She sat directly behind me. I could smell her budding sexuality…feel her dark Italian breasts penetrate into my body.

WALTER. Rosen?

ROSEN. My God, I haven't thought about Martha D'Angelo in years.

WALTER. Rosen! You're fucking with me and I don't like it.

ROSEN. They're only memories, Walter. They can't hurt you.

WALTER. If memories can't hurt us, then why do we need to talk to people like you.

ROSEN. To assure us that our memories are important.

(*He looks at his watch.*)

I like where we're going with this.

WALTER. I think you like it too much.

ROSEN. I get my pleasures where I can. We'll continue our remembrances of things past on Thursday.

(ROSEN *exits.* CARLOS *enters with a six-pack of beer. He sits down at table, pops open a couple of cans and hands one to* WALTER. *They tap cans and drink.*)

CARLOS. I've got some good news.

WALTER. What's that?

CARLOS. I talked to Annette. She wants to see you.

(no response from WALTER*)*

Aren't you glad?

WALTER. When does she want to see me?

CARLOS. In good time.

WALTER. But when?

CARLOS. Soon.

WALTER. Next week? The week after?

CARLOS. July. Early July.

WALTER. That's three months away.

CARLOS. It's just a better time for Annette.

WALTER. What's so special about July?

CARLOS. It's just better.

WALTER. Talk to me, Carlos.

CARLOS. *(avoids* WALTER*'s gaze)* The kids will be away in summer camp. Things will be quiet around the house. It's better when it's quiet.

WALTER. You mean it's better because Anna will be away.

CARLOS. Not just Anna but her younger brothers, Anthony and Aaron. They're good boys but a little wild. Every July we pack them off to summer camp. It's in the middle of Pennsylvania. They love it. And the house is so quiet.

WALTER. Tell Annette I'm busy in July. Very bad time.

CARLOS. C'mon, Walter.

WALTER. You should see my appointment book. It got crazy.

CARLOS. It's not what you think.

WALTER. Isn't it?

CARLOS. The important thing is that you and Annette must talk. She needs to see you, and you need to see her.

WALTER. I'm not a monster.

CARLOS. You're a good man, Walter. Okay, you once did some wrong things, but inside you're a good, decent man.

(**WALTER** *walks away from* **CARLOS**.)

WALTER. Maybe I'm not a good man. Maybe inside I'm bad, and I'll always be bad.

CARLOS. Don't talk like that.

(pause)

Next week Annette is going away for a few days. She's visiting a college friend in Baltimore.

WALTER. So she still keeps in touch with Leslie.

CARLOS. Yeah. The thing is that when Annette's away…I get horny as hell for other women. I mean I have fantasies about raping some beautiful woman.

WALTER. You don't have to tell me this.

CARLOS. I'm just talking, man.

WALTER. Carlos, I never raped a woman.

CARLOS. I know, I know. I'm just saying I understand.

(He stares into audience.)

It's crazy out there. Young girls wearing mini this and mini that. Sometimes when I walk down the street and pass some sexy-looking woman, she makes me feel like I'm bothering her. The bitch is staring down like she's afraid to look at me. Why she do that? Why can't she look me in the face?

WALTER. Maybe because you're looking in her face.

CARLOS. I see a pretty woman, I look. That's the price of beauty, my friend. Men will always look at a pretty woman. You ever see a man look at an ugly woman? And do you think an ugly woman is happy about that?

(pause)

I think if God were truly merciful He would cast a spell on the earth once a year. For one day each year a miracle would occur. All the ugly women in the world would look beautiful in the eyes of men, and all the beautiful women would look ugly.

WALTER. What about the women in between?

CARLOS. They'd look the same, naturally.

WALTER. Okay, what happens the day after this miracle?

CARLOS. Next morning there'd be a lot of shocked men when they turn over in bed.

(CARLOS laughs. WALTER looks at him.)

WALTER. Carlos, can I ask you something?

CARLOS. Sure.

WALTER. Did you ever…

(shakes his head)

Nothing.

CARLOS. Ask me. Ask me anything, man.

WALTER. *(pause)* How was Anna's birthday party?

CARLOS. It was great. I wish you could have been there. Anna looked like a princess. Annette fixed her hair real nice, and she wore a pretty red dress. There must have been thirty kids there. She's got a lot of admirers, let me tell you.

WALTER. Sounds like a good party. I wish I could have been there too.

CARLOS. I took pictures. You want to see?

WALTER. Another time.

CARLOS. I brought some with me.

(He reaches into his back pocket.)

WALTER. No!

CARLOS. What?

WALTER. No pictures! I don't want to see any pictures.

CARLOS. They're just photos I took of the party…Anna, her friends, one of Annette. I mean, maybe they're not Sports Illustrated, but they're nice photos.

WALTER. Carlos, I want to see my sister and your kids in person. Okay? Tell Annette I'll wait. All right? July will be fine. You tell her.

CARLOS. I'll tell her. Thanks, Walter.

(CARLOS exits. WALTER goes over to the table, opens drawer, and gets his notebook. He sits.)

WALTER. Kirby? What's hell like? Can't be any worse than state pen, right? Me? I ain't doing so good, but then I ain't doing so bad either.

(He writes.)

I wonder how Candy is doing? Haven't seen him in a week, ever since he took the cherub for a drive. Think he got scared? No, not the cherub. Candy. I've seen the cherub – next day. He looked all right, as if nothing had happened. Maybe Candy lost his nerve. Maybe it was just show and tell time...this time. I know what he's thinking about...I know his fears...his rationals ... his future. I almost feel sorry for the poor sonofabitch.

(He closes notebook and puts it away in table drawer.)

*(*NIKKI *enters.* WALTER *looks surprised.)*

NIKKI. Hi there.

WALTER. Hi.

(pause)

I didn't think you were coming back.

NIKKI. Why not?

(He gives her a shrug.)

What?

WALTER. You've been avoiding me at work.

NIKKI. I was giving you space.

WALTER. You gave me a lot of space.

NIKKI. Space is important.

WALTER. Don't need to tell me that.

NIKKI. So...how you been?

WALTER. *(points to beer on table)* I got beer. You want a beer?

NIKKI. It's eleven o'clock in the morning.

WALTER. It's also Saturday. You want beer?

NIKKI. I'd love a beer.

*(*WALTER *hands her one and takes one for himself.)*

Also, I didn't want to give the other guys any ideas.

(They pop open cans and drink.)

WALTER. What kind of ideas?

NIKKI. What do you think?

WALTER. I don't know.

NIKKI. Do I have to spell it out?

(WALTER just looks at her.)

You know.

WALTER. Better spell it out.

NIKKI. I put out for one, I'll put out for everyone.

WALTER. I haven't said a word.

NIKKI. I just didn't want to give them ideas.

WALTER. Maybe this isn't a good idea.

NIKKI. What?

WALTER. Us seeing each other.

NIKKI. Why's that, Walter?

WALTER. Should I spell it out?

NIKKI. You're scared.

WALTER. I'm not scared!

NIKKI. Neither am I.

WALTER. Maybe you should be.

(He turns away from her.)

NIKKI. I got an idea, Walter.

(WALTER seems somewhere else.)

Are you listening?

WALTER. Yeah.

NIKKI. We should live together.

WALTER. Live together.

NIKKI. Right.

WALTER. Here?

NIKKI. No, stupid. Move in with me.

(He stares at her.)

Walter, it's gonna take you years before you find another woman like me. I know this for a fact.

WALTER. Nikki, it's a bad idea.

NIKKI. I think it's a fucking good idea.

WALTER. I don't even know how to live with myself.

NIKKI. Just think about it.

WALTER. I've got problems.

NIKKI. Who doesn't?

WALTER. Most people don't have my kind of problems.

NIKKI. Guess that makes you pretty special.

WALTER. That's not what I meant.

NIKKI. I like you, Walter.

WALTER. The odds are against me.

NIKKI. What odds?

WALTER. You know, the percentages.

NIKKI. You lost me.

WALTER. For men like me…most of us end up back there.
The odds aren't good. In fact, they're rotten. That's
what I'm saying. I'm saying there are risks seeing me. I
say we call it quits. I'm sorry.

NIKKI. Excuse me.

(She exits.)

WALTER. She's gone!

(pause)

That was easy. Good. I'm glad. I'm fucking glad!

(stands up)

She was trouble too…big trouble. I knew that right
away. This is the best thing that could happen. Damn
right. Damn straight.

(picks up her beer can)

Damn! She could of at least finished her beer.

(NIKKI *reenters holding a potted plant.)*

You're back.

NIKKI. I left it downstairs.

WALTER. What is it?

NIKKI. What's it look like?

WALTER. Is it real?

NIKKI. Are you real? Shit, I knew you would never get one yourself.

WALTER. I don't need a plant.

NIKKI. Everyone needs a plant.

(She hands plant to **WALTER.***)*

This ivy is one tough baby. It's a cutting from one of mine. My oldest and favorite ivy. You okay with this?

*(***WALTER** *seems at a loss.)*

Here's the deal. Give it a little water. Go easy on the direct sunlight. And notice it every once in a while. I don't expect you to talk to it, though an occasional "good morning" wouldn't kill you. They love it when you look at them or touch their leaves. Can you handle that?

(He gives the plant a dubious look.)

I told you about my place. Horrible light. But I'll tell you this. Despite the odds, my plants grow. I have plant friends who swear it's a miracle. Don't tell me about odds, mister. Odds are bullshit.

WALTER. Thank you.

NIKKI. I think I need a little more attention than that.

*(***WALTER** *sets plant on table. Then he takes her in his arms and kisses her.)*

WALTER. Better?

NIKKI. After we make love, I'll tell you how I survived as the youngest and only daughter in a family of three sons. You wanna talk about odds?

WALTER. Maybe you should talk about it now.

NIKKI. Maybe not.

WALTER. Scared?

NIKKI. Give me another beer.

(He hands her one. She opens can and drinks. He waits.)

I got poked around...here and there.

WALTER. Which one?

NIKKI. Which one what?

WALTER. Which brother did this?

NIKKI. All three – in chronological order. As soon as one was old enough to date the next one got interested.

WALTER. Why are you telling me this?

NIKKI. You're such an asshole. I trust you.

WALTER. That the only reason?

NIKKI. I need more?

WALTER. Did Rosen call you?

NIKKI. Who's Rosen?

WALTER. Because if you're trying to – if you're trying to get me to – to confess – you can forget it! Understand? You can just forget it!

NIKKI. Walter, I'm not trying to get you to do anything. I'm trying to tell you who I am…if you're interested.

WALTER. Jesus. You must hate your brothers' guts.

NIKKI. I love my brothers.

WALTER. No you don't.

NIKKI. I love all of them. They're strong, gentle men with families of their own. And if you asked them about what they did to me, they'd call you a liar and then beat the shit out of you.

WALTER. You mean…you've never asked them about it?

NIKKI. *(laughs)* Are you serious?

WALTER. Not ever?

NIKKI. Not ever and not a word.

WALTER. Why?

NIKKI. It was a long time ago. It's over. Did it affect me? Maybe. Probably. But I couldn't tell you how.

WALTER. I bet you could.

NIKKI. I don't think so.

WALTER. Maybe you never tried.

NIKKI. You going to drag it out of me?

WALTER. I might.

NIKKI. I'll meet you in the torture chamber.

WALTER. Give me a second to find my hood.

(**NIKKI** *starts to exit then turns to* **WALTER**.)

NIKKI. Hey, I never told that to anyone before.

(*She exits to bedroom.* **WALTER** *collects the beer cans and takes them upstage. Returning, he stares at plant.*)

WALTER. Hello, plant. Welcome to my nightmare. Later I'll introduce you to Kirby.

(*He takes plant downstage. As he's about to set it on floor by window, he sees something outside.*)

What the hell is he doing?

(*to plant*)

See what I see? Candy's back. Right down there. But it's Saturday. And he's standing around like it's a Tuesday. Maybe he's starting to lose it...or maybe he's waiting for someone.

(*He looks a little to the right.*)

Yep. Here comes the cherub. Look at the smile on Candy. Look at Candy take the cherub by the hand. Look at Candy and the cherub disappear into...

(**WALTER** *backs away from the window and exits. The sound of birds chirping can be heard. A moment later* **ROBIN** *enters. She wears faded jeans and a baggy jacket. A pair of binoculars hangs from her neck. She looks through the binoculars.* **WALTER** *enters wearing a black denim jacket. He gazes at the girl. Long pause.* **ROBIN** *notices* **WALTER**.)

ROBIN. Hello.

(**WALTER** *is silent.*)

What are you looking at?

WALTER. Birds.

ROBIN. (*indifferently*) There's a million birds here.

WALTER. In that birch tree is a nest.

ROBIN. *(interested)* Where?

WALTER. *(points)* Up there.

> *(She looks through her binoculars. **WALTER** stares at her.)*

A little higher.

ROBIN. There's little chicks!

> *(turns to **WALTER**)*

You want to see?

WALTER. Sure.

> *(She hands him her binoculars. He looks through them.)*

ROBIN. They're starlings.

WALTER. Is that right?

ROBIN. I don't like starlings.

WALTER. Why not?

ROBIN. They're extremely aggressive birds. Other birds tend to stay away from them. Plus, their habits are rather filthy.

WALTER. The mother sure has her hands full.

> *(He hands her back the binoculars.)*

You always carry these?

ROBIN. When I go bird-watching. It's why I like coming here.

WALTER. It's just a city park.

ROBIN. You'd be surprised how many kinds of birds you'll see here. Last week I saw a purple martin. The week before that I saw a solitary vireo. That's rare.

WALTER. A solitary vireo. I like that one.

ROBIN. Their sound is quite musical.

WALTER. How does it sound?

ROBIN. It's hard to describe.

WALTER. Try.

ROBIN. I can't.

WALTER. I bet you can.

(**ROBIN** *shakes her head.*)

I'd love to hear it.

ROBIN. *(pause)* It's a bright sound.

(*She closes her eyes and pipes.*)

Cheery! Cheerily! Cheery! Cheerily!

(*She opens her eyes, shyly.*)

Something like that.

WALTER. That was terrific. I've never heard anything like it.

ROBIN. You should hear the bird.

WALTER. You live around here?

ROBIN. Are you a bird-watcher too?

WALTER. Me? Nah. I'm more of a people watcher.

ROBIN. Were you watching me?

WALTER. Not at first. You were staring at the tops of trees so intently, I thought any second you would take off and fly.

ROBIN. I have to go.

WALTER. Okay.

ROBIN. My daddy likes me home before dark.

WALTER. It's good to listen to your daddy.

(**ROBIN** *runs off and exits. Bird sounds stop.* **ROSEN** *enters. He sits and watches* **WALTER**, *who hasn't moved since* **ROBIN** *left.*)

I followed a girl.

ROSEN. Sit down, Walter.

(**WALTER** *sits.*)

WALTER. Did you hear what I said?

ROSEN. Why do you think you followed her?

WALTER. I don't know.

(**ROSEN** *writes in his notepad.*)

It was a fucking impulse, okay?

ROSEN. Did she know that you were following her?

WALTER. I don't know.

ROSEN. What did you think would happen?

WALTER. I don't know.

ROSEN. What did you want to happen?

WALTER. I don't know!

> (ROSEN *writes.*)

I can't believe I took such a risk.

> (*He glares at* ROSEN.)

Will you stop writing in that fucking pad?

> (ROSEN *stops.*)

ROSEN. All right.

WALTER. You know that if anything happens, anything, it means I spend the rest of my life in prison. No parole, no nothing. Just steel bars and death.

ROSEN. Is this the first one?

WALTER. Of course it is! That's why I'm telling you!

ROSEN. I'm glad you're telling me, Walter.

WALTER. You're such a bullshit artist, Rosen. You know that?

> (*mimics*)

I'm glad you're telling me, Walter.

> (ROSEN *is silent.*)

What should I do?

ROSEN. What do you want to do?

WALTER. Short of jumping off a bridge I don't know! That's why I'm asking you!

ROSEN. I want you to calm down and listen.

> (*With effort* WALTER *settles down.*)

WALTER. I'm okay.

ROSEN. You followed a girl. One girl. Perhaps you wanted to see what it felt like after so many years. You followed her and nothing happened. And here you are talking about it with me. This is healthy. This is progress.

WALTER. For Christ –

(takes a deep breath)

I'm listening.

ROSEN. When you go home, write down all the reasons why you think you followed her.

*(**WALTER** waits for more, but **ROSEN** is silent.)*

WALTER. That's it?

ROSEN. *(checks his watch)* We're out of time. We'll talk more about it on Thursday.

WALTER. I want to talk about it now!

ROSEN. Go home, Walter.

WALTER. Remember when you asked me what my idea of normal was? Now I know! It's when I can see a girl, be near a girl, talk to a girl…and walk away. That's my idea of being normal.

ROSEN. We'll talk more on Thursday.

*(**ROSEN** exits. **WALTER** goes to table and gets out his notebook. He writes, stops, stares at page.)*

WALTER. Fucking Rosen! This ain't helping.

(He tosses notebook in table drawer, closes it, then paces nervously downstage.)

Why did I take that chance? What did I want to happen? Maybe I wanted nothing to happen. Yeah! And nothing happened!

(He laughs.)

And nothing fucking happened! Nothing fucking happened!

*(**LUCAS** enters. He is a large, middle-aged man in a gray, rumpled suit. As soon as **WALTER** sees him, he becomes quiet.)*

LUCAS. Hiya, Walter.

WALTER. Cop.

LUCAS. Sergeant Lucas.

(He flashes his badge.)

May I come in?

WALTER. You are in.

LUCAS. So I am. But I always like to ask.

(*He looks around the room.*)

WALTER. What's up?

LUCAS. You don't know?

WALTER. I have no idea.

LUCAS. I think you do.

WALTER. Why don't you just tell me?

(**LUCAS** *walks downstage.*)

LUCAS. Too much sun.

WALTER. What?

LUCAS. (*points to plant*) Your ivy. Too much direct sunlight. These plants don't like a lot of sun.

WALTER. They grow outside, don't they?

LUCAS. Sure they do. But outside they've got trees around them. The trees shade them from the sun. Of course the plants enrich the soil around the trees. One of nature's symbiotic relationships.

WALTER. You going to take me on a nature walk?

(**LUCAS** *gives him a cold grin.*)

LUCAS. Two days ago you took the number twelve bus from work. But instead of getting off at your normal stop, for some reason you stayed on. Why did you stay on the bus, Walter?

WALTER. I fell asleep. When I woke up I was confused and got off the wrong stop by mistake. I walked home.

LUCAS. You walked home.

WALTER. That's right.

LUCAS. Why didn't you wait for the next bus back?

WALTER. I felt like walking. It was a pleasant evening.

LUCAS. It was a gray, muggy, overcast day with a high pollen count. My sinuses were killing me.

WALTER. I love those kinds of days.

(LUCAS pokes WALTER's head.)

LUCAS. Don't be witty. We know every step you make.

WALTER. I haven't broken any laws.

LUCAS. Then you won't mind if I look around.

WALTER. I would.

LUCAS. Got something to hide?

WALTER. Doesn't everybody?

LUCAS. I could get a search warrant.

WALTER. If you could, you would have brought one today.

(LUCAS crosses upstage. His eyes rest on the table.)

LUCAS. Cherry?

WALTER. Yeah.

LUCAS. Very nice.

(He rubs the table's surface. WALTER freezes.)

Unusual design for a contemporary piece.

WALTER. It's not for sale.

(LUCAS bends down for a closer look.)

I said it's not for sale!

(LUCAS stands up.)

LUCAS. Who said I wanted to buy it?

(WALTER is silent.)

Yesterday a ten-year-old girl was attacked not far from here. Seems there's been a number of attacks on young women and girls in the general vicinity. Kind of a coincidence, wouldn't you say?

WALTER. What time did it happen?

LUCAS. I'll ask the questions.

WALTER. You're looking for more than one man.

LUCAS. What?

WALTER. Sex offenders either go after women or young girls – rarely both.

LUCAS. I guess you're an expert on the subject.

(He walks around the room.)

WALTER. I've done some reading. But then I had the time.

(He sticks his hands in his pockets.)

If you tell me when this happened perhaps I could clear up –

LUCAS. Move your fucking hands away from your pockets!

(WALTER does.)

Sit down!

(WALTER sits.)

We know every step you make, every goddamn step! We know when you sleep, when you eat, when you shit, and when you jack off.

(LUCAS looks into audience.)

And when you sit by the window, watching the girls in their little cotton skirts parade by. Do you wave your wanger at the girls? Is that when you jack off? Or do you do it quietly in the corner?

WALTER. You can't talk to me like –

LUCAS. A piece of shit? In my eyes you are a piece of shit. Think anyone would miss you if I threw you out the window right now? I could say you jumped when I came in. Who are they going to believe? Not you, because you'd be a dead piece of shit.

WALTER. What's your badge number? I demand to know your badge number!

LUCAS. My badge number is shut the fuck up!

(chuckles)

Heard that line once in an Al Pacino movie. I always wanted to use it. Of course, Pacino said it better.

(moves closer to WALTER)

We just want to make sure you're being a good boy. Okay?

(WALTER doesn't answer. LUCAS taps him on the forehead.)

Okay?

WALTER. Okay.

(LUCAS sits in a chair.)

LUCAS. Some of them walk right into a family's home. Walk in as if they live there. Very fucking ballsy. Or they climb through the bedroom window. And it's always when the parents are in another part of the house. Uncanny how they know this. Like a sixth sense. I've talked to these guys. They tell me things that make my neck hairs stand up.

(pause)

This one guy on death row, who I'll call Henry, told me about his last victim. Henry says how he's in the bedroom of a seven-year-old cutie named Adele. Her mother's in the living room watching TV. She's got the volume on so damn high he can hear David Letterman's jokes. Still, Henry puts his hand over Adele's mouth and says, "If you scream, little girl, I'll kill your mother." And of course little Adele doesn't scream, doesn't cry, doesn't make a sound. Then he takes her hand and out they go through the front door. Ten days later they find Adele's body. Or what's left of it.

(pause)

You believe in fairy tales, Walter?

WALTER. Fairy tales?

LUCAS. Do you believe in them?

WALTER. No.

LUCAS. Neither do I.

(pause)

What's the one with the woodsman?

WALTER. Woodsman?

LUCAS. Yeah.

WALTER. What woodsman?

LUCAS. The one with the axe.

WALTER. I don't know.

LUCAS. Sure you do. He cuts open the wolf's stomach, and the girl steps out alive.

WALTER. Little Red Riding Hood.

LUCAS. That's it! Little Red Riding Hood jumps out of the wolf's guts with hardly a scratch.

(pause)

Ever seen a seven-year-old girl sodomized almost in half?

*(**WALTER** is silent.)*

She looked so small and broken. I saw hardened twenty-year veterans cry. They cried like babies. I was there. Ain't no fucking woodsman in this world.

(He rises.)

I don't know why they keep letting scum like you return to the streets. It just means we got to catch you all over again.

*(He stands over **WALTER**.)*

The next time you fuck up will be the last time. Because I'll be there.

*(He slaps the back of **WALTER**'s head and exits. **WALTER** remains seated, but he can't hold back his tears.)*

WALTER. You have no right to talk to…to speak like…I am not!…I am not!…

*(**WALTER** drops to his knees. He crawls to table and takes out his notebook. He rips out a page and crumples it up. The **GIRL** enters.)*

GIRL. Wallie! What are you doing?

*(**WALTER** quickly stuffs page in his mouth. Blackout.)*

*(Spot on **ROSEN** sitting down stage.)*

ROSEN. Where are you, Walter?

(He looks at his watch.)

Don't do this to me.

(Spot out. Lights up on **WALTER**. *The* **GIRL** *is gone. He rocks back and forth in chair.)*

WALTER. God is a pedophile. God is a rapist. God is a murderer. God is a mass murderer. God is a torturer. God is a terrorist. God is an arsonist. God is a schizophrenic. God is a sadist. God is evil.

(He rips a page out of notebook, crumples it up.)

It's all in the Bible.

(He stuffs page in his mouth. Blackout. Spot on **ROSEN**.*)*

ROSEN. Shit.

(He throws his notepad down and exits. Spot out. Lights on **WALTER**.*)*

WALTER. God is a pedophile. God is a rapist. God is a murderer. God is a mass murderer. God is a torturer. God is a terrorist. God is an arsonist. God is a schizophrenic. God is a sadist. God is evil.

*(***NIKKI** *enters in black tank top and panties.)*

NIKKI. Walter, come to bed.

*(***WALTER** *murmurs same "God" speech.)*

What are you doing?

*(***WALTER** *continues murmuring.)*

Walter! You're scaring me!

(She exits. Blackout.)

(Spot on **ROSEN** *speaking in phone.)*

ROSEN. Hello? Yes. This is Rosen. Who is this? Who? He what?

(listens)

I'm sorry, I can't. I'm very busy. I don't do – Then why didn't he – This is not – Calm down.

(looks at his watch)

All right. I'll be there. Six o'clock?

(Blackout. Lights up. **NIKKI** *and* **ROSEN** *are at the*

table, sitting across from each other.)

NIKKI. Thanks for coming over.

   (**ROSEN** *looks around.)*

ROSEN. Rather Spartan.

NIKKI. Walter thinks he's still in prison.

ROSEN. Walter didn't tell me he had a girlfriend.

NIKKI. It probably slipped his mind.

ROSEN. Slipped his mind?

NIKKI. We met at work…in the warehouse.

ROSEN. Oh?

NIKKI. He thought I was a dyke, then he found out I wasn't.

ROSEN. How did you get my number?

NIKKI. You're listed. You have a practice, right?

ROSEN. I mean how did you know to ask for me?

NIKKI. Walter mentioned your name.

ROSEN. You called me because he mentioned my name?

NIKKI. Walter talks about you. A lot.

ROSEN. He does?

NIKKI. He thinks you're a helleva guy.

ROSEN. He does?

NIKKI. I bet I heard him say it half a dozen times: "That Rosen, he's one fucking good guy." Or "Rosen is one brilliant sonofabitch." Or "Rosen is one bastard who really knows his shit."

ROSEN. One fucking good guy.

   (shakes his head)

Amazing. I always thought he looked down on me. Thought me a fool.

NIKKI. Nah.

ROSEN. I'm surprised. Stunned. It just shows that one should never make assumptions. Thank you, Nikki.

NIKKI. Mr. Rosen?

ROSEN. Call me Ira.

NIKKI. Ira.

ROSEN. God, I feel foolish. No, I feel ashamed.

NIKKI. Ira?

ROSEN. This has been a revelation. I hope you'll forgive me
    for being –

NIKKI. Ira! Walter never said that.

ROSEN. What?

NIKKI. Walter never said those things about you.

ROSEN. But...

NIKKI. I'm real sorry.

ROSEN. Oh...But he did on occasion talk about me.

NIKKI. He did.

ROSEN. Can you tell me what he said?

NIKKI. I'd rather not.

ROSEN. *(tersely)* Why did you lie?

NIKKI. Because I want you to help me...to help Walter.

ROSEN. I tried to help him. But I can't if he won't see me.
    You know, I'm suppose to report to his parole officer if
    he misses an appointment.

NIKKI. Will you call?

ROSEN. I was going to give him one more day.

NIKKI. He's losing it, Ira. That's why you have to help him.

ROSEN. Can you be more specific?

NIKKI. He's all twisted up.

ROSEN. You mean he's stressed about something?

NIKKI. *(pause)* I think Walter's looking for a girl.

ROSEN. What do you mean?

NIKKI. What do you think I mean?

ROSEN. I'd rather you tell me.

NIKKI. I mean that Walter is out there looking.

ROSEN. Can you elaborate?

NIKKI. I'm afraid he'll get in trouble...that...

ROSEN. That he'll molest a minor?

NIKKI. Yeah.

ROSEN. How do you know Walter's looking?

NIKKI. You haven't seen him lately. Today he didn't show up for work. I was able to put in an excuse for him, but if he misses another day without calling…

ROSEN. What can I do about it?

NIKKI. Help me stop him.

ROSEN. We can't stop him if he's driven to do that.

NIKKI. You gotta car, I gotta car. Let's go find him.

ROSEN. I am a therapist not a detective.

NIKKI. If he does something and they catch him, they'll put him away for life!

(She starts to cry.)

ROSEN. You really care about him, don't you?

NIKKI. Walter's a good man. I know he is!

ROSEN. Listen, Nikki. I can't force my patients to behave, to "do the right thing." In the end it's up to them. I'm sorry.

NIKKI. Is that how you treat your patients?

ROSEN. Nikki.

NIKKI. That is one fucked-up methodology!

ROSEN. You're not being fair.

NIKKI. What's the suicide rate among your patients? I bet it's pretty damn high. They must drop off like fucking flies.

ROSEN. Good-bye, Nikki.

(He gets up to leave.)

NIKKI. Yeah. So long, Ira. Thanks for your understanding.

(turns on him)

Walter said you were an incompetent twerp! He said you're full of shit! He said you couldn't cure a mosquito of hunger if you were buck naked!

ROSEN. Getting me angry is not going to make me help you.

NIKKI. Then why the fuck are you still here?

ROSEN. *(He looks at her for a long moment.)* My car's across the street.

NIKKI. Thank you.

(They exit. Blackout.)

*(Lights up. **WALTER**, wearing his jacket, sits on a park bench – two chairs pushed together. The sound of birds chirping is heard. **ROBIN** enters. The binoculars hang from her neck. She looks at **WALTER**, who stares upward.)*

ROBIN. See anything interesting?

WALTER. Not yet.

*(**ROBIN** sits on the other end of the bench. From her jacket pocket she takes out a small book and starts writing in it. **WALTER** watches her.)*

I've seen you write in that book before.

ROBIN. It's my bird book.

(She shows him the book.)

I've identified sixty-seven species of birds this year alone.

WALTER. Sixty-seven. That is impressive.

*(**ROBIN** writes in her book.)*

Where are your friends?

*(**ROBIN** doesn't answer.)*

Don't you have friends?

ROBIN. I have friends.

WALTER. A pretty girl like you should have a lot of friends.

ROBIN. I'm not pretty.

WALTER. Well...not in a common way.

(She stops writing.)

ROBIN. What does that mean?

WALTER. Means uncommon beauty is commonly overlooked. Most people only notice birds with the brightest colors.

ROBIN. I never thought of that.

WALTER. What's your name?

(**ROBIN** *writes in her book.*)

Linda…Susan…Jennifer…Kimberly…

(**ROBIN** *continues writing, but she smiles.*)

You tell me your name, I'll tell you mine.

ROBIN. *(pause)* Robin.

(**WALTER** *laughs.*)

Yeah, like the bird. But it's really a family name. My mother's favorite aunt was named Robin. But I never knew her cause she died young in a car crash when a drunk teenager in a Ford pickup hit her Honda head on. She was only thirty-six and quite beautiful. It was very tragic. My mother named me after her.

WALTER. Robin. I think it suits you.

ROBIN. So do I.

WALTER. Can I ask you how old you are?

ROBIN. I'm twelve.

WALTER. No you're not.

ROBIN. I will be twelve in three months. I can't wait. I hate being eleven. It's got to be the stupidest age in the world. I mean, just look at the number.

(She puts her two index fingers together.)

Two dumb straight lines standing stupidly next to each other.

(pause)

What's your name?

WALTER. Walter. No story. My folks just liked the name.

ROBIN. Do you have many friends?

WALTER. No.

ROBIN. How come?

WALTER. A long time ago, I was sent far away. When they let me come back, all my friends were gone.

ROBIN. It sounds like you were banished.

WALTER. Banished…You could say that.

ROBIN. Birds are my friends. That sounds egotistical, but they are. Birds know I watch them, but they don't mind because they like being watched...if they know you won't hurt them.

WALTER. Robin?

ROBIN. Yes?

WALTER. Would you like to sit on my lap?

ROBIN. What?

WALTER. Would you like to sit on my lap?

ROBIN. *(pause)* No thank you.

WALTER. Are you sure?

ROBIN. Yes.

WALTER. You don't sound sure.

ROBIN. I'm sure. Thank you all the same.

WALTER. That's okay...doesn't matter.

ROBIN. *(pause)* Do you want me to sit on your lap?

WALTER. Yes. I would enjoy that.

ROBIN. Why do you want me to...

WALTER. Because I like you. And we can talk better.

(He slides closer to **ROBIN***.)*

ROBIN. Talk about what?

WALTER. Like why do you watch birds.

ROBIN. Because they're not like any kind of animal. It's like there are people and there are animals...and then there are birds.

*(***WALTER** *touches* **ROBIN***'s shoulder. She closes her eyes.)*

Maybe it's because they live in the sky and not on the earth...or that they're covered with feathers and not with hair or that they make music and not just sounds when they speak.

(His fingers brush **ROBIN***'s hair. She shudders.)*

WALTER. Are you cold?

*(***ROBIN** *shakes her head.)*

You look cold.

(She is silent.)

Robin, I know a place in the park where only very small birds go. There are no people or dogs or ugly crows and pigeons. It's quiet except for the song of these tiny sparrowlike birds. Would you like me to take you there?

ROBIN. They sound like finches.

WALTER. They could be finches. I don't know. We should go before it gets dark.

(He stands up.)

Ready?

*(**ROBIN** doesn't move.)*

ROBIN. My daddy lets me sit on his lap.

WALTER. Does he?

ROBIN. Yes.

WALTER. Do you like it when he asks you?

ROBIN. No.

*(Her answer has a strange effect on **WALTER**, as if for a moment he lost his balance. Carefully, he sits down and stares at his hands.)*

WALTER. Why not?

*(**ROBIN** is silent.)*

Are you two alone when he asks you?

(still silent)

Does he touch you?

(She looks through the binoculars.)

Does he say strange things?

(She scans the trees.)

Does he move his legs in a funny way?

*(**ROBIN** drops her head and quietly sobs. **WALTER** looks at her but offers no comfort.)*

Have you told your mother?

(She shakes her head.)

You don't want to tell your mother?

(She shakes her head.)

Is there anyone at home you can talk to?

(She is silent.)

Is there a teacher you like at school?

(She nods.)

What's her name?

ROBIN. Ms. Kramer.

WALTER. Tell Ms. Kramer what your daddy does.

ROBIN. I can't.

WALTER. Yes you can, Robin. You said you couldn't make the sound of a solitary vireo. But you did. Beautifully. I heard you.

ROBIN. What will happen if I do?

WALTER. Someone will talk to your daddy. And then he'll stop doing those things to you…the things you don't like.

ROBIN. But will he…

WALTER. Your daddy will always love you.

ROBIN. Are you sure?

WALTER. Yes.

ROBIN. How do you know?

WALTER. I know because…it's just something I know.

ROBIN. I don't want to hurt my daddy.

WALTER. Robin? Listen to me.

(He struggles with the words.)

At first he'll be upset…very upset…because he'll realize he's been a bad daddy. Then he'll try…He'll try very hard to be a good daddy…People will say stupid, ignorant things about your daddy. That will be hard for you…But one thing I know for sure, he'll always love you…always.

ROBIN. Walter?

WALTER. Yes?

ROBIN. You still want me to sit on your lap? I will. I don't mind.

(*WALTER slides away from her.*)

WALTER. No.

ROBIN. I want to.

WALTER. You should go home.

ROBIN. Can't I stay a little longer?

WALTER. Go home.

ROBIN. Will I see you tomorrow?

WALTER. No.

ROBIN. Will I ever see you?

WALTER. I can't...see you.

ROBIN. Why?

WALTER. I'm going away. But I'll always remember you, Robin.

(*ROBIN gets up, goes over to WALTER, and hugs him. WALTER remains still.*)

ROBIN. Good-bye.

(*She runs off. WALTER covers his face and breaks down. When he takes his hands away, he notices the binoculars on the bench. He looks over to where ROBIN left.*)

WALTER. Hey! You left your...

(*He picks up the binoculars and stares at them. Black-out.*)

(*spot on ROSEN on phone*)

ROSEN. He's back? When did he get – Has he said any – Yes, Nikki, I'm glad he's back...Tell him I said to – What? He has a special message for me? What is it?

(*pause*)

He'll see me on Thursday.

(*brief smile*)

Tell him...I'll be waiting.

(spot out)

(Lights up. **WALTER** *folds a shirt on the table where a small pile of clothes lie. He puts the folded shirt in a cardboard box on the floor by his feet. Upstage is another cardboard box.* **LUCAS** *enters. He walks casually upstage and glances at the cardboard box. He crosses to the table.)*

LUCAS. Hiya, Walter. May I come in?

WALTER. Have a seat, Sergeant Lucas.

LUCAS. I'll stand.

WALTER. What can I do for you?

(He continues folding clothes.)

LUCAS. Can you tell me where you were last night?

WALTER. I was here. Why?

LUCAS. Just answer my questions. You were here all night?

WALTER. That's right.

LUCAS. You never left the apartment?

WALTER. I said I was here.

*(***LUCAS** *crosses downstage and looks into the audience.)*

LUCAS. Last night a man was badly beaten across the street. You know anything about that?

WALTER. No.

LUCAS. You hear anything unusual? screams? shouts?

WALTER. I was asleep.

LUCAS. *(pause)* I didn't say what time the assault occurred.

WALTER. You said last night. I went to bed pretty early. And my window was closed.

LUCAS. The assault took place at approximately seven-thirty.

WALTER. I went to bed around seven.

*(***LUCAS** *gives him a skeptical look.)*

I wasn't feeling well.

LUCAS. I could take you downtown.

WALTER. You could. It'd be a waste of your time. Got any witnesses?

(**LUCAS** *looks around.*)

Right, you're asking the questions.

LUCAS. There was a boy there.

(**WALTER** *is silent.*)

He I.D.'d the assailant. The description matches you pretty well.

WALTER. I suppose if you're looking for a Caucasian male between the ages of thirty and fifty, medium height, medium weight, medium build. Probably not too many men fit that bill.

LUCAS. Just give me a straight answer, Walter, cause the irony goes right over my head.

WALTER. I told you I was asleep.

LUCAS. The boy said this man was wearing a black denim jacket.

WALTER. How could he tell the jacket was black if it was night.

LUCAS. Who said it was dark? Who said they were outside?

WALTER. You said it was across the street. The only place across the street is the school. School's closed at night.

LUCAS. You own a black denim jacket?

WALTER. No. Denim reminds me of prison attire.

LUCAS. Mind if I look around?

WALTER. I don't mind – if you have a search warrant.

LUCAS. *(pause)* That's a nasty scratch on your neck.

WALTER. *(touches the side of his neck)* This? I have a very passionate girlfriend.

LUCAS. Then I'd say you're a lucky man.

WALTER. I count my blessings before I go to bed.

(**LUCAS** *walks around.* **WALTER** *folds another shirt.*)

LUCAS. What's with the boxes?

WALTER. You're a cop. Figure it out.

LUCAS. I'd say you're moving.

WALTER. It's a free country, isn't it? Just kidding.

LUCAS. Again with the irony.

WALTER. I'm moving in with my girlfriend.

LUCAS. The passionate one?

WALTER. I need a change of scenery.

LUCAS. Good idea.

> *(pause)*

Well, guess I'll be going.

WALTER. Think you'll catch this guy?

LUCAS. Oh, yeah. We'll catch him.

WALTER. That's good.

LUCAS. Unfortunately, the victim can't talk. In addition to his other injuries, his jaw is broken.

> (**WALTER** *is silent.*)

However, we ran an I.D. on the victim. Turns out he's wanted in Pennsylvania. He raped a boy there.

> (**LUCAS** *watches* **WALTER**, *who impassively rolls a pair of socks.*)

You might say this assailant did us a favor. You sure you don't know anything about this?

WALTER. 'Fraid not. And I don't do favors for cops.

LUCAS. Stay out of trouble, Walter. Cause I'll be watching you.

> *(He goes to exit.)*

WALTER. Lucas.

LUCAS. Yeah?

WALTER. How's the boy?

LUCAS. He'll survive.

WALTER. Was he…

LUCAS. Just stay out of trouble.

> (**LUCAS** *exits.* **WALTER** *tosses the socks in the box.* **NIKKI** *enters in a rush.*)

NIKKI. You ready to go? My car's double-parked.

WALTER. I'm ready.

NIKKI. You can change your mind.

WALTER. *(smiles at her)* I am ready.

NIKKI. Good. Cause I'd of killed you if you changed your mind.

(**WALTER** *kisses her then holds her to him tightly.*)

Hey, we'll have plenty of time for that later.

(She touches his face.)

I'll make sure there's time.

WALTER. Let's go. We'll start with the boxes. Then we'll come back for the table and plant.

(He throws rest of clothes in box while she goes to the box upstage.)

NIKKI. Where's your jacket? It's cold outside.

WALTER. I'm all right.

(They lift their burdens. **NIKKI** *exits first.* **WALTER.** *starts to exit when the* **GIRL** *enters.* **WALTER** *stops. The sound of children fades in.)*

GIRL. Wallie!

(**WALTER** *faces the* **GIRL.***)*

You forgot me.

WALTER. No...I didn't forget.

(He puts the box down and takes a step toward her. The **GIRL** *opens her arms. He takes another step. She moves slowly toward him until they're very close.)*

GIRL. Oh, Wallie.

(He reaches for her.)

NIKKI *(Offstage)* Walter?

(**NIKKI** *enters. The sound of children stops. The* **GIRL** *runs out.)*

NIKKI. What happened to you?

(**WALTER** *doesn't move.*)

Walter?

(He reaches into the box and takes out a pair of binoculars.)

WALTER. I thought I forgot these.

(pause)

I watch birds.

NIKKI. Birds?

WALTER. A recent interest. I want to expand...my interests.

NIKKI. Walter, I don't know about you.

(She picks up the plant.)

But I guess I'll find out.

*(She exits. **WALTER** picks up the box. He takes a look around.)*

WALTER. In time.

(He exits. Lights fade to spot on table then blackout.)

COSTUME PLOT

WALTER: Khaki pants, flannel shirt, work shoes
GIRL: Nightgown
ROSEN: Sport coat, slacks, button down shirt, loafers
CARLOS: Working clothes
NIKKI: Black jeans, black tank top, black leather jacket, heavy work boots
LUCAS: Gray suit
ROBIN: Faded jeans, long-sleeved top, jacket, tennis shoes

PROPERTY LIST

3 wooden straight back chairs
Small cherry wood table with drawer
Bottle of red wine (half full)
6-pack of can beer (domestic)
Potted ivy plant
Binoculars
Police sergeant's badge in wallet
Notebook
Notepad
Journal book filled with handwriting and bird drawings
3 pens
2 coffee mugs
2 cardboard boxes
Small pile of clothes (2 assorted men's shirts and 3 pair of socks)

SET DRAWING

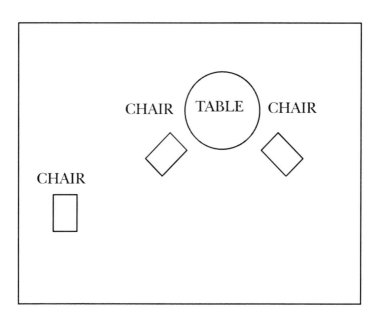

LaVergne, TN USA
02 September 2009
156649LV00001B/9/P